Arthur

I l l u s t r a t e d   b y   D o n n a   G y n e l l

Arthur was a very ordinary dog.
He lived in Mrs. Humber's Pet Shop
with many other animals,
but Arthur was the **only** dog.
All the other dogs
had been sold because
dogs were very popular—
all the dogs **except Arthur.**
He was just
an ordinary brown dog,
who dearly wanted a home,
with a pair of old slippers to chew.

阿瑟是一隻很普通的小狗。
他住在韓媽媽寵物店，
和許多動物在一塊。
但是阿瑟卻是唯一的小狗。
其他的狗
全都賣出去了，
因為人們都喜歡小狗，
除了阿瑟以外。
他只是一隻
普普通通的黃狗，
渴望有個家，
有雙舊拖鞋可咬。

On Monday morning Mrs. Humber
put some rabbits in the window.

By the end of the day
the window was empty,
except for Arthur.
Nobody wanted an
ordinary brown dog.
Everybody wanted rabbits.

So that night,
when all was quiet,
Arthur practised being a rabbit.

星期一早上，韓媽媽
在櫥窗裡放了幾隻兔子。

一天過去了
櫥窗裡的兔子全都賣光，
只剩下阿瑟。
沒有人想要一隻
平凡的黃狗。
大家都想養兔子。

所以那天晚上，
當一切都安靜無聲時，
阿瑟練習學做兔子。

He practised eating carrots
and poking out his front teeth
and making his ears stand up straight.

He practised very hard
until he was **sure**
he could be a rabbit.

他練習吃胡蘿蔔、
露出門牙，
還試著把耳朵豎起來。

他很努力地練習著，
直到他確信
自己可以當隻兔子。

Next morning Mrs. Humber
put some snakes in the window.

By the end of the day
the window was empty,
except for Arthur.
Nobody wanted an
ordinary brown dog,
not even one
who acted like a rabbit.
Everybody wanted snakes.

So that night,
when all was quiet,
Arthur practised being a snake.

隔天早上，韓媽媽
放了幾條蛇到櫥窗裡。

一天過去了，
櫥窗裡的蛇也全都賣光，
只剩下阿瑟。
沒有人想要一隻
普通的黃狗，
無論他多會模仿兔子。
大家都想養蛇。

於是那天晚上，
趁著四周靜悄悄的時候，
阿瑟練習學做蛇。

He practised hissing
and slithering and sliding
and looking cool.

他ㄊㄚ試ㄕ著ㄓㄜ發ㄈㄚ出ㄔㄨ嘶ㄙ嘶ㄙ聲ㄕㄥ、
扭ㄋㄧㄡ曲ㄑㄩ著ㄓㄜ身ㄕㄣ子ㄗ及ㄐㄧ滑ㄏㄨㄚ動ㄉㄨㄥ，
還ㄏㄞ裝ㄓㄨㄤ出ㄔㄨ一ㄧ付ㄈㄨ很ㄏㄣ酷ㄎㄨ的ㄉㄜ樣ㄧㄤ子ㄗ。

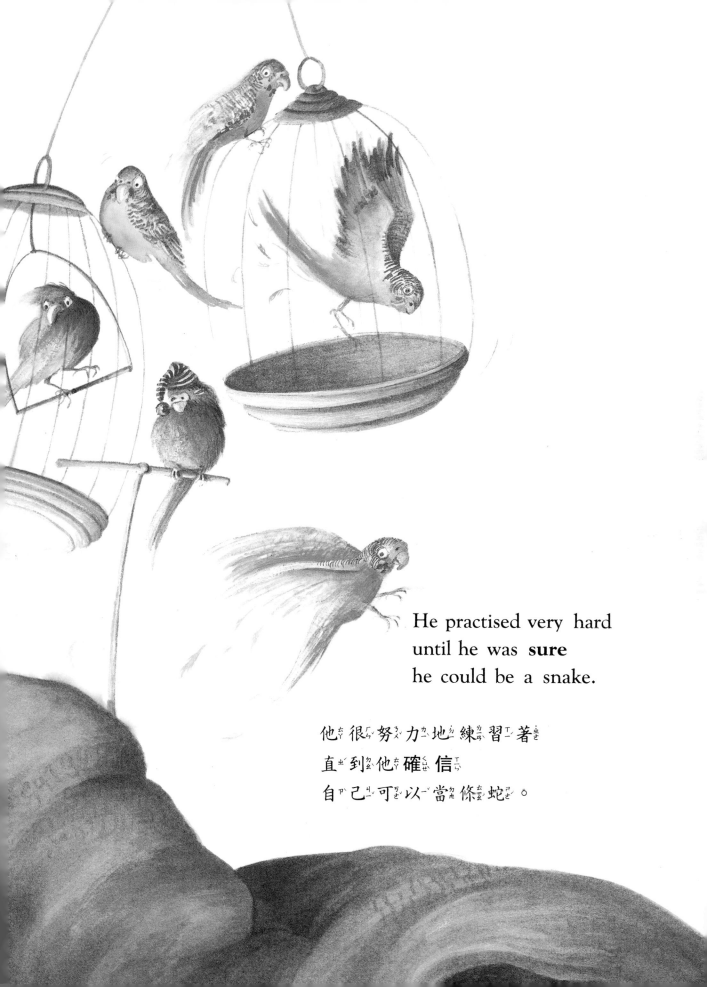

He practised very hard
until he was **sure**
he could be a snake.

他很努力地練習著
直到他確信
自己可以當條蛇。

Next morning Mrs. Humber
put some fish in the window.

By the end of the day
the window was empty,
except for Arthur.
Nobody wanted an
ordinary brown dog,
not even one
who acted like a rabbit and a snake.
Everybody wanted fish.

So that night,
when all was quiet,
Arthur practised being a fish.

隔天早上，韓媽媽
又在櫥窗裡
放了幾尾金魚。

一天過去了，
櫥窗裡的金魚全都被買走，
只剩下阿瑟。
沒有人想要一隻
長相平凡的黃狗，
無論他多會模仿兔子和蛇。
每個人都想養金魚。

所以那天晚上，
　趁著夜深人靜時，
　　阿瑟又練習學做金魚。

He practised swimming
and blowing bubbles
and breathing underwater.

He practised very hard
until he was **sure**
he could be a fish.

他練習游泳、
吐氣泡，
還有在水中呼吸。

他很努力地練習著，
直到他確信
自己可以當條金魚。

Next morning Mrs. Humber
put some cats in the window.

By the end of the day
the window was empty,
except for Arthur.
Nobody wanted an
ordinary brown dog,
not even one who acted
like a **rabbit**
and a **snake** and a **fish**.
Everybody wanted cats.

Arthur felt he would
never find a home
with a pair of old slippers to chew.

隔天早上，韓媽媽
在櫥窗裡
放了幾隻貓。

一天過去了，
櫥窗裡的貓全都賣光，
只剩下阿瑟。
沒有人想要一隻
普通的黃狗，
無論他多會模仿
兔子、
蛇，以及金魚。
每個人都想養貓。

阿瑟覺得自己
永遠也找不到家，
也沒有舊拖鞋可以咬了。

隔天早上，韓媽媽
把她剩下的寵物全放進櫥窗裡。
共有兩隻倉鼠、一籠老鼠、三隻金絲雀、
一隻藍色的虎皮鸚鵡、一隻綠蛙、
一隻懶洋洋的蜥蜴，還有阿瑟。

Next morning Mrs. Humber put the rest of her
pets in the window. There were two hamsters,
a cage of mice, three canaries, a blue budgerigar,
a green frog, one sleepy lizard and Arthur.

Arthur jumped on lilypads,
squeaked
and nibbled cheese,
purred, croaked
and even attempted to **fly.**

阿Y瑟ㄙㄜˋ跳ㄊㄧㄠˋ到ㄉㄠˋ荷ㄏㄜˊ葉ㄧㄝˋ上ㄕㄤˋ，
學ㄒㄩㄝˊ老ㄌㄠˇ鼠ㄕㄨˇ吱ㄗ吱ㄗ叫ㄐㄧㄠˋ、
小ㄒㄧㄠˇ口ㄎㄡˇ小ㄒㄧㄠˇ口ㄎㄡˇ地ㄉㄧˋ啃ㄎㄣˇ乳ㄖㄨˇ酪ㄌㄠˋ；
一ㄧˊ下ㄒㄧㄚˋ呼ㄏㄨ嚕ㄌㄨ地ㄉㄧˋ打ㄉㄚˇ呼ㄏㄨ，一ㄧˊ下ㄒㄧㄚˋ又ㄧㄡˋ呱ㄍㄨㄚ呱ㄍㄨㄚ叫ㄐㄧㄠˋ，
他ㄊㄚ甚ㄕㄣˋ至ㄓˋ還ㄏㄞˊ想ㄒㄧㄤˇ飛ㄈㄟ起ㄑㄧˇ來ㄌㄞˊ呢ㄋㄜ！

By the end of the day
the window was empty,
except for Arthur.

一天過去了，
櫥窗裡又是空盪盪的，
只剩阿瑟一個。

He had collapsed,
exhausted
in the corner of the window.

Now he was certain he would never
find a home,
whether he was a rabbit, a snake, a fish, a cat,
or a purple, spotty, three-headed wombat.
Arthur decided that he might as well
be just an ordinary brown dog.

他失望地倒下來，
筋疲力竭地
縮在櫥窗的角落。

現在，他確信自己
不可能找到新家了，
不管他是不是
兔子、蛇、金魚、花貓，或是
長滿斑紋的三頭紫袋熊。
阿瑟決定自己還是
做一隻平凡的黃狗算了。

Late that afternoon,
just before Mrs. Humber
was to close the shop,
a man came in with
his granddaughter.
"Excuse me," said the man,
"Melanie tells me that
you have a rather
extraordinary dog,
who performs all sorts of tricks."
"The only dog I have,"
replied Mrs. Humber,
"is Arthur."

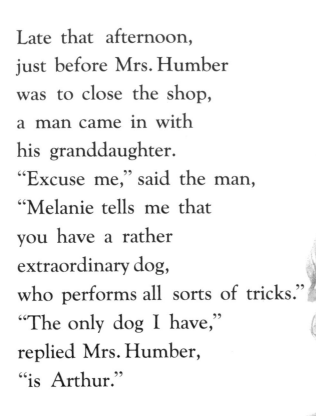

那天傍晚，
就在韓媽媽要打烊前
有一位老先生帶著
他的孫女走進店裡。
老先生說：「打擾了，
梅蘭妮告訴我，
你們這裡有一隻
很特別的狗，
會耍各種特技呢！」
韓媽媽說：
「我這裡唯一的狗
就是阿瑟啊。」

"**There** he is Grandpa,
in the window!" said Melanie.
She rushed to pick up Arthur,
who gave her the
biggest, wettest, doggiest lick ever.

Arthur knew he had found a home,

「老爹，他在那兒，
就在櫥窗裡！」梅蘭妮大喊著。
她衝過去抱起阿瑟，
阿瑟用小狗最撒嬌的方式
熱情地舔溼梅蘭妮的臉頰。

阿瑟知道自己已經
找到了新家，

with a pair of old slippers to chew.

也_{ㄧㄝˇ}有_{ㄧㄡˇ}舊_{ㄐㄧㄡˋ}拖_{ㄊㄨㄛ}鞋_{ㄒㄧㄝˊ}可_{ㄎㄜˇ}咬_{ㄧㄠˇ}嘍_{ㄌㄡ}。

恭禧阿瑟
終於有個新家！
想知道阿瑟
是怎麼學會做家事
以及
他又怎麼會離家出走嗎？
趕緊看精彩的續集
《阿瑟做家事》
和
《永遠的阿瑟》吧！！

國家圖書館出版品預行編目資料

阿瑟找新家:我愛阿瑟 I / Amanda Graham,
Donna Gynell著; 三民書局編輯部編譯.
－－初版三刷.－－臺北市: 三民，2006
　　面；　　公分

ISBN 957-14-2524-9　（精裝）

859.6

網路書店位址　http://www.sanmin.com.tw

© 　阿瑟找新家
　　　──我愛阿瑟 I

著作人　Amanda Graham　Donna Gynell
編譯者　三民書局編輯部
發行人　劉振強
著作財
產權人　三民書局股份有限公司
　　　　臺北市復興北路386號
發行所　三民書局股份有限公司
　　　　地址／臺北市復興北路386號
　　　　電話／(02)25006600
　　　　郵撥／0009998-5
印刷所　三民書局股份有限公司
門市部　復北店／臺北市復興北路386號
　　　　重南店／臺北市重慶南路一段61號
初版一刷　1997年1月
初版三刷　2006年1月
編　號　S 853441
精裝定價　新臺幣貳佰元整
平裝定價　新臺幣壹佰陸拾元整
行政院新聞局登記證局版臺業字第○二○○號